For Oscar
and Amy

# MILTON AND THE BIG FREEZE

WRITTEN BY TONY GARTH
ILLUSTRATED BY IAN JACKSON & TONY GARTH


Typography and typesetting - Metcalf & Poole, Leeds, England.

Microscopic Milton had just finished his breakfast of one cornflake dipped in warm milk and was ready for a new and exciting day with his friend Douglas.

Milton lived in an old clock on the mantelpiece above the fire so of course it was always lovely and warm inside, even on the coldest of winter mornings.

Milton dressed and walked to the edge of the mantlepiece to find Douglas who was as usual sleeping in front of the fire below.

Milton was about to say good morning when he happened to glance out of the window.

'Wow!' he shouted! it's been snowing. Look Douglas'.

Douglas woke from his nap and looked out of the window. Sure enough the whole garden was completely covered in snow.

'It's wonderful,' said Milton, 'lets go outside and throw snowballs.'

Douglas liked the snow, but only from the inside of a warm and cosy room, nevertheless he agreed to play with Milton and they headed for the kitchen door.

In the kitchen, Mrs Witherspoon had just baked yet another batch of mince pies.

'You can never have enough mince pies,' she would always say. 'You never know when someone may call in for a cup of tea,' and off she went to the shop to buy flour and eggs so that she could make even more.

'Keep an eye on things Douglas,' she called 'and when I get back, one of those pies will be yours'.

Douglas loved mince pies.

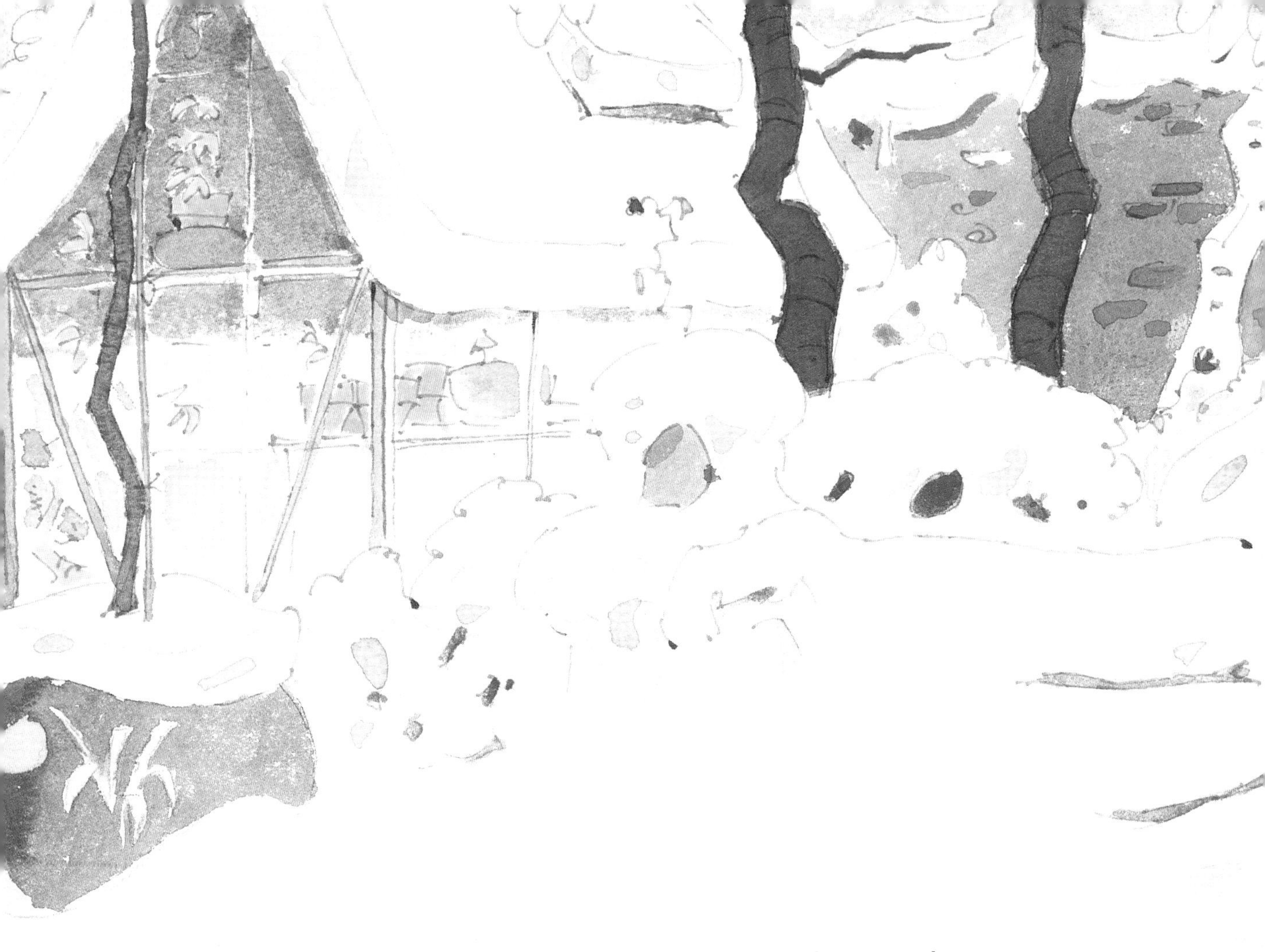

Milton and Douglas stepped out into the garden. The snow was quite deep and came right up to Douglas' knees but when Milton stepped into it he disappeared completely. Douglas bent his head so that Milton could climb onto the end of his nose. 'L-l-let's f-find a sh-shallower place to play,' shivered Milton and off they went to investigate.

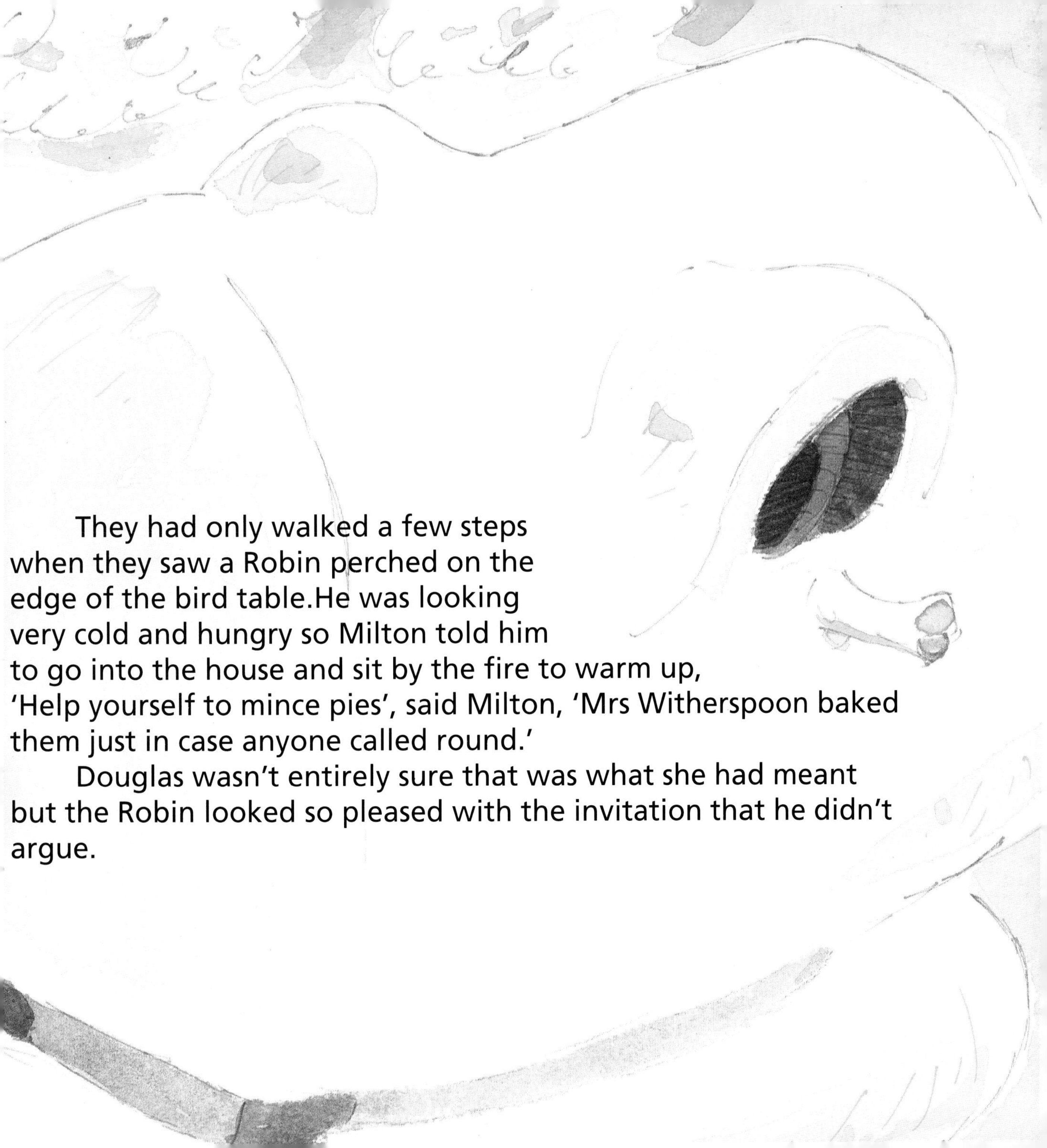

They had only walked a few steps when they saw a Robin perched on the edge of the bird table.He was looking very cold and hungry so Milton told him to go into the house and sit by the fire to warm up, 'Help yourself to mince pies', said Milton, 'Mrs Witherspoon baked them just in case anyone called round.'

Douglas wasn't entirely sure that was what she had meant but the Robin looked so pleased with the invitation that he didn't argue.

The Robin flew into the house and Milton and Douglas continued to look for somewhere to play.

'What's that strange noise?' asked Milton, who had heard a sort of clicking sound, 'it's coming from the hold in the oak tree.' Douglas lifted Milton up to the hole. He peered inside to find two squirrels huddled together to keep warm but it didn't seem to be working as the noise he had heard was the chattering of squirrel teeth.

'You poor things', said Milton, 'go into the house where it's warm and have something to eat.'

The squirrels looked very grateful and bounded across the snow and into the house.

'It seems that winter isn't fun for everyone Douglas', said Milton as they looked into the fish pond which was covered in thick ice. 'Those poor goldfish', he thought and had an idea. Milton and Douglas went back to the kitchen to fetch one of the hot mince pies and placed it on top of the ice.

'The pie will melt the ice', explained Milton, 'and then fall through into the water so that the goldfish can eat it.'

'Very clever', thought Douglas who was enjoying the smell of the hot mince pie and looking forward to eating his own when Mrs Witherspoon came back from the shop.

Douglas wasn't the only one enjoying the smell. All over the garden birds and animals were peeping out from their hiding places and sniffing the air.

'They all look so cold and hungry', thought Milton and before Douglas could stop him he had invited every last one of them (and all their family and friends) into the house.

Just then it began to snow again and a snowflake landed right on top of Milton's head, to someone his size it was like being hit by a snowball.

'Brr!' he said 'I think I've had enough of snow for one day, let's go inside where it's warm.'

When Milton and Douglas opened the parlour door they couldn't believe their eyes. The room was completely filled with animals and birds of all shapes and sizes and they all looked very happy indeed now that they were warm and full of Mrs Witherspoon's delicious mince pies.

Milton was very pleased with himself for doing such a good deed but Douglas was beginning to get rather worried, the house was full of wildlife and all the pies were gone.

Douglas put his front paws on the window sill and looked out across the garden. Through the gap in the trees he saw a bus stopping at the end of the road and Mrs Witherspoon climbing off.

'Woof!' he shouted and Milton and the animals took this to mean 'quick! everyone out of the house, Mrs Witherspoon is back.'

Milton and Douglas quickly rounded up the animals and led them through the kitchen and out into the garden. The last one to leave was the Robin who flew back onto the bird table just as Mrs Witherspoon opened the garden gate.

'I've just seen a robin', she said to Douglas as she came into the kitchen, 'you don't usually see much wildlife at this time of year.'

'You should have been here two minutes ago', thought Milton as he crept quietly back to his clock.

Mrs Witherspoon put down her shopping. 'Now Douglas', she said, 'I promised you a mince pie didn't I.' She turned to the kitchen table where she had left them to cool. To her surprise they were all gone, not even a single crumb was left.

'Well!' she said. 'It looks as though you've had more than your fair share already you greedy dog.'

'But I haven't even had one,' thought Douglas as he walked sadly back into the parlour and lay down by the fire.

'I was really looking forward to that pie', thought Douglas.

'Never mind', said Milton as he disappeared around the back of his clock, only to reappear pushing a mince pie. 'I saved one for you.'

Milton pushed the pie over the edge of the mantle piece and Douglas gobbled it up in a flash.

'I saved it from last Christmas,' added Milton, 'I never have liked mince pies.'

Douglas didn't seem to mind and stretched out in front of the fire for another nap.

'Roll on Spring', he thought.